I dedicate this book to Josh and Jimmy who were a big help

in getting it done, and as always, to all my grandchildren.

*Vanita Oelschlager*

ACKNOWLEDGMENTS

Kristin Blackwood
Mike Blanc
Kurt Landefeld
Paul Royer
Sheila Tarr
Jennie Levy Smith
Elaine Mesek
Josh Shade
Jimmy Longton
Kelly Fogel
Barb Darbutt
Shelly Drage
Carolyn Brodie
Michael Olin-Hitt
Steve Cosby
Gailmarie Fort

**A Tale of Two Daddies**
VanitaBooks, LLC

Text by Vanita Oelschlager
Illustrations by Kristin Blackwood and Mike Blanc
Design by Jennie Levy Smith,
Trio Design & Marketing Communications, Inc.
Printed in the USA
Hardcover Edition ISBN 978-0-9819714-5-2
Paperback Edition ISBN 978-0-9819714-6-9

www.VanitaBooks.com

# A Tale of Two Daddies

by **Vanita Oelschlager**
*illustrations* **Kristin Blackwood**
*and* **Mike Blanc**

VanitaBooks, LLC

My friend Lincoln says
you have two dads.

That's right.
*Poppa* and *Daddy*.

Who's your dad when your hair needs braids?

Who's your dad when you're afraid?

*Poppa's* the one when I need braids.

*Daddy* is there when I'm afraid.

Which dad would build your house in a tree?

And which dad helps when you skin your knee?

*Poppa's* the one who builds in a tree.

*Daddy's* the one who fixes my knee.

Which dad helps when your team needs a coach?

Which dad cooks you eggs and toast?

*Daddy* is my soccer coach.

*Poppa* cooks me eggs and toast.

Who's the dad who helps with homework?

And which dad helps when you're covered with dirt?

*Both* my dads help with my math.

But *Poppa's* the dad who helps in the bath.

Which one makes your birthday cake?

Who is the one who stays up late?

*Daddy* makes my birthday cake.

*Neither* one likes to stay up late.

Which dad helps you with the litter box?

Which dad helps you match your socks?

*Poppa* helps clean kitty's litter box.

And *I'm* big enough to match my own socks.

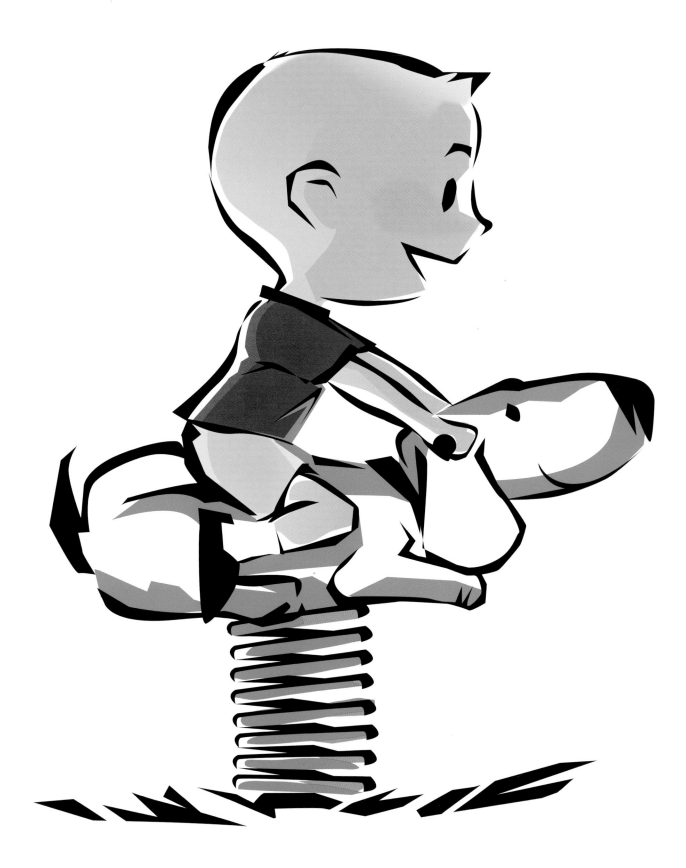

Who's your dad when chasing your dog?

Who's your dad for catching some frogs?

*Neither* dad can catch my dog.

But *both* of them can catch a frog.

Which dad helps when your day begins?

Who is there to tuck you in?

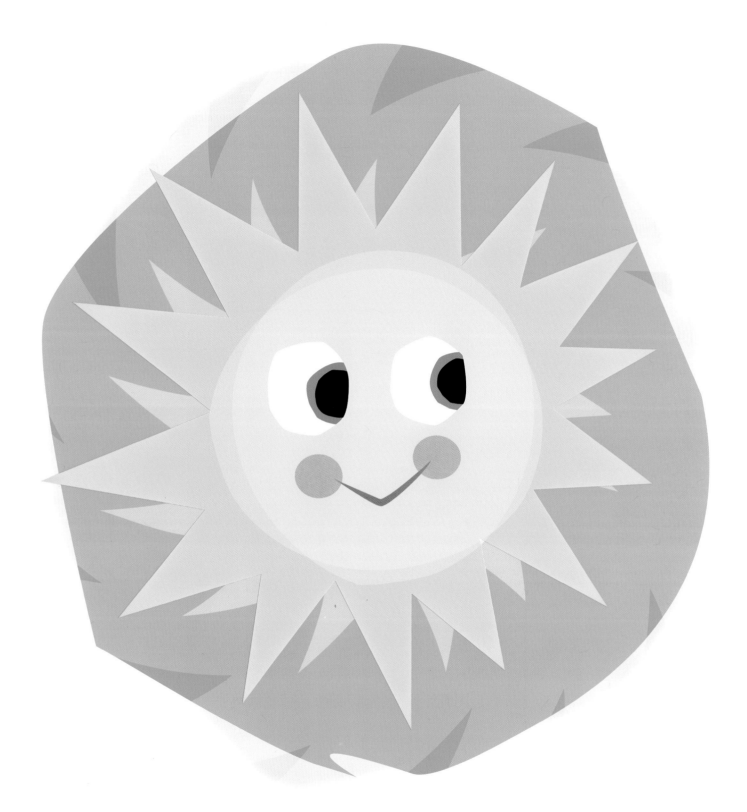

*Poppa's* awake when my day begins.

*Both* of my daddies tuck me in.

Who is your dad when you're sad and need some love?

*Both*, of course.

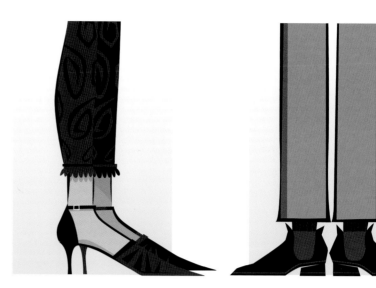

### Vanita Oelschlager

is a wife, mother, grandmother, philanthropist, former teacher, current caregiver, author and poet. A graduate of Mount Union College in Alliance, Ohio, she now serves as a Trustee of her alma mater and as Writer in Residence for the Literacy Program at The University of Akron. Vanita and her husband Jim were honored with a *Lifetime Achievement Award* from the National Multiple Sclerosis Society in 2006. She was the Congressional *Angels in Adoption* award recipient for the State of Ohio in 2007 and was named *National Volunteer of the Year* by the MS Society in 2008. Vanita was also honored in 2009 as the *Woman Philanthropist of the Year* by the Summit County Chapter of the United Way.

### Kristin Blackwood

is a teacher and frequent illustrator of books for children. Her works of art are published in: *My Grampy Can't Walk, Let Me Bee, What Pet Will I Get?, Made in China, Big Blue, Ivy in Bloom* and *Ivan's Great Fall.* A graduate of Kent State University, Kristin has a degree in Art History. When she isn't designing or teaching, she enjoys being a mother to her two daughters.

### Mike Blanc

is a life-long professional artist. His work has illuminated countless publications for both corporate and public interests worldwide. Accomplished in traditional drawing and painting techniques, he now works almost exclusively in digital media. His first book, *Francesca*, was written by Vanita Oelschlager and published in autumn 2008. Their second collaboration, *Postcards from a War*, was released in 2009.

Step 1

Step 2

Step 3

Step 4

## About the Art

The artwork for *A Tale of Two Daddies* was developed and produced in four steps. First: Kristin and Mike established the characters through pencil sketches that were refined in editing sessions as the story developed. Drawings for each page were scanned into computers to form templates. Second: The artists used Adobe® Illustrator® vector-editing software to plot each shape needed to build the illustration using curve and corner points that were then adjusted, converting each sketch to a computerized version. Third: Every shape was assigned a color attribute based on the book's color palette. Last, the template was discarded and the image was fine-tuned with softening effects and transparency. Once complete, the illustrations were gathered into sequence within the larger book design of the finished work: *A Tale of Two Daddies*.

## Profits

All net profits from this book will be donated to charitable organizations, with a gentle preference toward those serving people with my husband's disease – multiple sclerosis.

**Vanita Oelschlager**

VanitaBooks, LLC